MUSCLE

BOUND

other books in the series

Beating Up Daniel
After Dinner Barf
Dear Liz
Dangerous Rivals

BAYVIEW HIGH

MUSCLE BOUND

H.A. Levigne

Vanwell Publishing Limited
St. Catharines, Ontario

This book is a work of fiction. Names, characters, places, and incidents are the product of the author's imagination. Any resemblance to actual persons, living or dead, is entirely coincidental.

Vanwell Publishing Limited   **In the United States**
P.O. Box 2131   P.O. Box 1207
1 Northrup Crescent   Lewiston, NY
St. Catharines, ON   USA 14092
Canada L2R 7S2
sales@vanwell.com
1-800-661-6136

Produced and designed by Tea Leaf Press Inc.
www.tealeafpress.com

Design: Jane Lewis
Editorial: Kate Calder, April Fast,
                 Jane Lewis, and Hannelore Sotzek

Printed in Canada

National Library of Canada Cataloguing in Publication

Levigne, Heather, 1974-
     Muscle bound / Heather Ann Levigne.

(Bayview High)
ISBN 1-55068-116-8
ISSN 1702-0174

     I. Title. II. Series.

PS8573.E96438M88 2002   jC813'.6   C2002-901216-3
PZ7

For John,
with all my love

chapter 1

busting out

Kalen Sommers turned his father's red pickup truck into the parking lot at Bayview High. The early morning sun was just breaking over the old brick high school. A few cars were parked near the entrance. Kalen cut the engine and stepped out of the truck. He grabbed his gym bag from the seat beside him. He stretched his arms and ran his hand through his blond hair.

Today was the first basketball practice of the season. Every August, Coach Nesbitt held preseason practices. The basketball team practiced for two weeks. By the time school started, the team was well prepared for the opening game of the season. Kalen felt the excitement growing in his stomach. He was looking forward to hitting the court.

It was Kalen's third year at Bayview High. He was a good athlete and student. He wasn't bad-looking, either—the girls loved his surfer-blond hair, green eyes, and shy smile.

A car horn blared behind him, making him jump. Shielding his eyes against the sun, Kalen turned to see his best friend, Scott Jansen, pulling into the parking lot. Kalen grinned and began walking toward the car. Scott and Kalen had been best friends since the fourth grade. Of the two boys, Kalen was the calm, cool one. Scott was more outgoing and impulsive.

Scott never seemed to sit still. He played basketball for the Bayview Sharks—he was a forward, and Kalen played guard. Scott also played football and was on the track-and-field team. Last year, Scott began to feel that people thought he was a jock. He joined the debate team to prove them wrong. He surprised everyone when he was voted captain of the team. Even though he was busy, Scott always had time for fun.

"Hey, man! How was your summer?" Scott said as he jumped out of his battered blue Jeep and slammed the door. "How was the lake?"

Kalen smiled. "Great, as usual," he replied. "Lots of swimming, canoeing, fishing…you know how it is."

Every summer, Kalen went to Crooked Lake with his family. Mr. Sommers was a teacher, so he had summers off. Mrs. Sommers was a social worker. She was taking a leave of absence from work to write a book. She brought her laptop with her everywhere she went. She even brought it to the cottage. She just put on some sunscreen and her floppy beach hat. Then she propped her computer in her lap and worked while she sat on the deck.

Kalen's jaw dropped in shock when he saw Scott. "Scott! What the heck have you been doing all summer? You're...you've got..." Kalen stopped. He was stunned. Scott looked totally different. Over the summer, his body had changed completely. Even though he wore a thick sweatshirt, Kalen could see that Scott's neck, arms, and shoulders bulged with muscles. He looked like one of the guys in *Musclebound Magazine*. Kalen couldn't believe his eyes. Scott had always been the little guy on the team. Now he was built like a weightlifter.

"Oh, it's nothing...I've been working out, that's all. I'm taking some protein supplements and stuff to bulk up. I'm just getting ready for basketball season." He flexed his right arm. "And maybe for the girls, too," he said with a big grin.

Kalen stared at Scott's bulging biceps. He shook his head in disbelief. "Are you kidding? You're *ripped!* Look at your arms and shoulders, man! Coach Nesbitt is going to freak when he sees you."

Scott grabbed his bag out of the back of the Jeep and slammed the lid. "Okay, okay, that's enough. My head will swell if you keep it up. I won't fit through the door! Let's go before we miss practice."

"Never mind your head, Scott, your *shoulders* may not fit through the door," Kalen muttered under his breath. He followed Scott into the building.

Practice was long and tough, but Kalen felt good afterward. It was great to get back on the basketball court. After showering, Kalen pulled a hooded sweatshirt over his head. "Hey, Scott, where did you get those protein supplements? I was thinking about checking them out myself," he said, his voice muffled.

"Here, man—catch." Scott tossed Kalen a copy of *Musclebound Magazine.* "Everything you need is in that magazine. The back section is full of ads for protein powders, pills, whatever. You can order them straight from the company."

Kalen flipped through the magazine. "So how do you know what to use?" he asked.

Every page seemed to advertise a magic powder or pill for bigger, harder, leaner muscles. There were so many choices that it was overwhelming.

Scott took an oversized plastic bottle from his bag. It was labeled "FAT BLASTERS" in big red letters. "At first I was ordering from the magazine, but now I get most of my stuff from my gym. I get a discount when I order in bulk. The manager used to be a bodybuilder, so he knows what works and what doesn't," he said. Scott handed the bottle to Kalen. "So, like, this stuff is for burning fat. I take two pills at every meal. They help speed up my metabolism, so my body burns fat faster and builds more muscle. I'm eating way bigger meals now. I eat more often, too. I have to watch what I eat, though, or I'll get fat. "

"I don't think I have a problem burning fat," Kalen said, looking down at himself. His body was long and lean. "It's the muscle part I need."

"That's what workouts are for," Scott replied. "I go to the gym three days a week—three days on and two days off. Listen, I'm starving. Do you want to grab a burger at Lee's? I could use some protein." Scott was sitting on a bench, tying his shoe.

Kalen looked puzzled. "Why do you need so much protein?" he asked.

"All the pro bodybuilders eat a lot of protein. That's what builds muscle," Scott explained.

Kalen began to reply, but he was interrupted by a loud clang. A locker slammed shut next to him. A tall, good-looking boy with dark hair stood smirking down at Scott.

"You'll need more than burgers if you want to make starting line this year," said the dark-haired boy. "Like, a miracle."

Seth Morgan was a year older than Kalen and Scott. He was *always* bullying them, especially Scott. Scott had always been one of the smallest guys on the team. Seth seemed to enjoy picking on Scott especially. Seth was usually with his buddies, Russ Daniels and Matt Webb. They were always bragging about being the best players on the team. Kalen wasn't looking forward to another year on the same team as those guys.

Scott looked up quietly. His face was calm. "I suggest you back off, Morgan, if you don't want any trouble," he said. There was an edge in Scott's voice.

Seth laughed. "Oh, really? Are you threatening me, Jansen?" he sneered. His friends moved in and crowded Scott.

Kalen took a step forward, but Scott was already on his feet. The locker room had suddenly gone quiet. All eyes had turned toward Scott and Seth.

Seth's eyes widened as he took in Scott's wide shoulders and muscular arms. Seth laughed, but Kalen thought he sounded slightly nervous. "Well, well, you've grown over the summer, Jansen," Seth scowled. He narrowed his dark eyes at Scott. "You're almost as wide as you are tall...what's that, about four, maybe five feet now?"

Scott's blue eyes flashed furiously. He took a step toward Seth but stopped at the sound of Coach Nesbitt's voice. "Listen up, all of you! I need all eyes on me before you go."

Scott turned away from Seth. He and Kalen walked toward the group of guys gathering around the coach. Seth hissed, "We'll finish this conversation later, Jansen." Scott ignored him.

Coach Nesbitt stood with his hands in the pockets of his faded track pants. He wore a blue tracksuit with "Bayview Sharks" in white letters across the shoulders. He was about forty-five years old. Years of coaching high school basketball made him look about fifteen years older than he really was.

Coach Nesbitt waited for the room to become quiet. "First of all, I want to congratulate you on a great first practice. I think

13

we've got a great team this year," he said gruffly. "I can tell that many of you were practicing during the summer." He glanced up from his clipboard and looked at Kalen. "Sommers, your lay-up has really improved. Good job! We need to work on passing a little more, though."

The coach cleared his throat. "I want you all to know that it's been hard to choose the starting lineup for this season," he said. "There's a lot of talent on this team. Don't worry if you don't see your name on the list next week. It doesn't mean you won't get any court time. You're all going to get a chance to show your stuff. Just keep practicing. Look to your senior teammates for pointers. We've got to work together to take home the Championship Cup this year!"

chapter 2

pass the protein

It was past four o'clock by the time Kalen and Scott left Lee's Restaurant. They had spent most of the afternoon hanging out at Lee's. Kalen had his favorite—a hamburger loaded with cheese and pickles, and fries with gravy. Scott usually ordered the same thing. Today, he ordered a burger with no bun and a salad on the side. "I can't eat all that fat anymore," he said to Kalen.

Maybe I should cut out some fat, too, Kalen thought to himself.

Afterward, Kalen drove home. He parked the pickup truck in the driveway of the Sommers' home at 16 Cherrytree Street. He hopped out of the truck and ran up the front steps. A fat orange tabby cat jumped down from an old wicker loveseat on the porch.

"Hey, Ginger," he said, reaching down to scratch the cat behind her ears. She wound herself around his legs, purring loudly. Kalen picked up the newspaper from the front steps. He walked into the house, whistling to himself.

"Hellooo! Anyone home?" Kalen called, tossing his keys on the table in the front hallway.

"In here," his mother replied. She was seated in front of the computer in the Sommers' home office. It was really only an office when Mrs. Sommers was using it to work on her book. The rest of the family used the computer mostly for e-mail and playing games.

Today, Mrs. Sommers was sitting in front of the computer. Her glasses sat on top of her head. Stacks of books lay open around her. She was going through some papers in her lap.

Kalen's mother looked up and smiled at him as he walked into the room. "Hi, honey. How was practice?"

"Fine," Kalen replied. He collapsed into an easy chair. "I'm starving. What's for dinner?"

"Um…I'm not sure. I think your father may be making lasagna," Mrs. Sommers said. Her eyes were glued to the computer screen as she typed. "Why don't you invite Amber over for dinner? She hasn't been here in a while. We'd love to see her."

Amber Johnston was Kalen's girlfriend for the last six months. They had started seeing each other last year. Since Kalen had been away at Crooked Lake for the summer, he hadn't seen her very much lately. Kalen e-mailed her from his mother's laptop while he was at the cottage. It wasn't the same thing as talking to her in person. Kalen thought about Amber's beautiful brown eyes and her warm laugh. A big smile spread over his face.

His mother saw his goofy grin. "I'll bet Amber missed you a lot, hmm? You spent a lot of time checking your e-mail while we were at the cottage," Kalen's mom said. A smile tugged at the corners of her mouth.

"I don't know...yeah...probably," Kalen said. His face turned red. "I'll call her and see if she wants to come over tonight."

Mrs. Sommers chuckled under her breath. "Okay. Let your dad know we are having an extra person for dinner tonight, please." She turned back to the computer and kept typing.

Kalen fiddled with a loose thread on his pants. "Sure. Hey, Mom," he said suddenly, "I think I might join a gym so I could work out after school. Just to, like, build some muscle or something. Bulk up a bit. I'm so *skinny* compared to the rest of the guys on the team."

Mrs. Sommers glanced at Kalen. "What do you mean you are *too skinny?* You are perfectly healthy. Why would you want to *bulk up?*"

"Well, Scott has been working out all summer, and you should see him now, Mom! He's huge!"

His mother shook her head. "I don't know, Kalen. How will you have time to work out? You're already very busy with school, basketball, and work. Remember our agreement," she warned.

Kalen sighed. "Yeah, I remember," he said.

When Kalen started high school, his parents had told him that his schoolwork had to come first. "It's easy to get caught up in girls and sports," his father had said. "We know you need to relax and have fun, but your education is important, son. You need to balance school and fun. You can play *one* sport, and you can have a part-time job to make some spending money. If your schoolwork starts to suffer, you'll have to give up one or the other."

So far, the agreement was working. During the week, Kalen had basketball games and practices after school. On the weekend, he worked at Howard's Grocery Store. He stocked shelves and bagged groceries. Saturday nights were free for hanging out with his friends. He also spent a lot of time with Amber.

Kalen looked hopefully at his mother. "Mom, working out is important to me. It'll only take up one more hour of my time. I'm not working at the store that much. I can go to the gym on Friday night and Saturday afternoon after I get off work. It won't interfere with school," he promised.

Mrs. Sommers sighed. "Okay, Kalen. You can give it a try. But I don't think you should worry too much about being muscular. You're only seventeen years old. Give your body time to finish growing up."

Kalen kissed his mother on the cheek. "Thanks Mom! Don't worry," he said happily.

He decided to find out more about Scott's workout routine and new diet as soon as possible. At school, Kalen had seen lots of guys his age who had bigger biceps and better abs than he had. What if Amber decided to check out those guys? Kalen didn't want that to happen. He decided to start a serious workout program by the end of the week.

chapter 3

take one scoop
of jealousy...

"**C**ome on, Kalen, settle down," Amber giggled. She playfully pushed Kalen away. "I'm trying to watch TV!"

The two teens were relaxing in front of the TV after dinner. Kalen kept tickling Amber's ears and neck, trying to distract her from the show she was watching. Ever since he'd met Amber, Kalen had a crush on her. Amber was smart, pretty, and funny. Kalen was crazy about her. He thought she was the prettiest girl at Bayview High.

Amber had long, thick red hair and big brown eyes. She had a sprinkling of freckles across her nose. Like Kalen, Amber was an athlete. She played volleyball and soccer at Bayview High. She also wrote articles for the school newspaper, *The Bayview Post*. Last year, she wrote a story about students buying essays on the Internet. Miss Roth, the advisor for the paper, thought Amber's story was really good. She sent it to the local newspaper. The newspaper printed it on the front page!

Kalen flopped back against the sofa cushions and sighed. "I've had enough TV," he groaned. He jumped to his feet and walked into the kitchen. "Do you want a snack?" he called.

"More food? We just finished dinner," Amber replied. She grabbed the remote control.

"Yeah, but I need something to eat. I need to gain some weight," Kalen said. He opened the refrigerator and looked inside.

"What for?" Amber asked.

"Well, I was reading this article that Scott gave me. It was about building muscle. It says you have to eat more in order to build muscle. I could use some muscle. Look at my arms," Kalen said in disgust. "They're puny. I have *no* definition in my abs, either. I need to bulk up!" He grabbed a carton of cottage cheese from the fridge.

Amber sat up. She tipped her head to one side and looked at Kalen. "I don't see anything wrong with your arms," she said finally. A playful look came into her eyes. "In fact," she continued, "I think they're perfect. Why don't you come back over here and give them a workout? I could use a hug."

"Seriously, Amber. Don't you think I'd look better with more muscle? I'm so tall and skinny. I look like a beanpole. I want to get started on a workout program before school starts," Kalen said. "Scott says I could stand to gain another twenty pounds. He said that I should only eat certain foods, too." Kalen pulled a piece of paper from his back pocket. "Scott has been drinking this protein shake. Here's the recipe."

"Can I see that?" Amber took the note. "What's 'creatine'?" she asked, reading the ingredients on the recipe.

Kalen shrugged. "I don't know, but Scott says it helped him get into great shape. I figure I should drink it three times a day and work out four days a week. I should be able to gain twenty pounds of muscle in six weeks."

Amber looked doubtful. "Where did you say Scott got this recipe?"

"Um…*Musclebound Magazine*, I think. The protein powder is called MegaMass 4000. I can order it right from the magazine. I can also order it on the Internet at www.megamass.com."

Amber handed back the recipe. "Well, I think you look great just the way you are. If you want to get ripped, go ahead. Just be careful, okay?" Amber said.

Kalen put down his snack and sat on the couch next to Amber. He put his arm around her and pulled her close. "Hey, don't worry about it. Before you know it, you'll be dating the best-looking guy at Bayview High."

Amber looked up at him with an innocent look on her face. "Oh, really? And who might that be?"

"Oh, you're gonna pay for that one!" Kalen pounced on her. He tickled her until she gasped for mercy.

"*Aaaaahhhahahahaha!* Okay, I give, I give!" shrieked Amber, laughing.

chapter 4

join the club

The next Saturday afternoon, Kalen decided to visit some gyms in town. He checked the prices and hours of almost every fitness center. Some were too expensive, and others were for women only. Finally, he went to The Sweat Shop, which was where Scott worked out.

The Sweat Shop was a new gym with brand-new equipment. A lot of the members were serious bodybuilders. Scott had told Kalen that he had picked up some tips from them. Plus, Scott said he could buy protein supplements there. It definitely sounded worth checking out.

Kalen pushed open the double glass doors of The Sweat Shop. Instantly, a wave of warm, damp air washed over his face. It smelled strongly of sweat and lemon floor polish.

Inside, the gym looked new and modern. It had gleaming chrome fixtures, mirrored walls, black rubber benches, and mats on the floor. Through a glass door, he could see men and women using the exercise machines. Everyone was concentrating on their images in the mirrors.

Kalen saw Scott leaning on an exercise bike. He was talking to a heavily muscled guy with a goatee. Kalen pushed open the glass door and walked toward them.

"Hey, Scott! What's up?" Kalen called.

Scott turned around, looking surprised. "Kalen! What are you doing here?"

"Just checking out your gym. I'm pumped for a workout," Kalen grinned. He flexed his arms and posed like a bodybuilder.

The guy with the goatee stared at Kalen.

Clearly, he has no sense of humor, Kalen thought. He dropped his arms.

"Later, man," the big guy said to Scott.

"What's his problem?" Kalen asked, glaring at the other guy. The bodybuilder just ignored Kalen. He sat down on a bench loaded with weights and began lifting.

Scott glanced around. "Karl's a pro. He takes this stuff seriously," he answered. "Hey, I'm finished here. I'll introduce you to Dan— he's the owner. Come on."

The boys walked toward a glassed-in office in the corner of the room. A well-built man was sitting behind a large glass-topped desk. Trophies lined a shelf behind the desk. A framed cover of *Musclebound Magazine* hung on the wall. It was a picture of a huge guy flexing his muscles. His arms were raised above his head. Kalen could see every muscle in his body. They were almost popping out of the picture.

The man stood up when Kalen and Scott stepped into the office. "Hey, Scott, how's it going? Have you tried the new leg press yet? It just arrived yesterday," he said. His blond hair was cropped short. His tight black t-shirt stretched across his massive chest and showed off his huge arms.

"Hey, Dan, this is my friend Kalen. He wants to join a gym. I told him The Shop is the best one in town," Scott said, grinning.

"Kalen! Great to meet you," Dan said. He grabbed Kalen's hand and gave it a firm shake. "Are you just starting out?"

Kalen looked embarrassed. "I guess it's pretty obvious, isn't it?" he said. He felt like a little kid next to Dan.

Dan clapped one big hand on Kalen's shoulder, nearly knocking him off balance. "Hey, it's no big deal. I wasn't always this big. It took a lot of hard work to build this body," he said with a smile.

"Dan used to compete all over the world," Scott explained. "He won the Mr. Ultimate Championship when he was twenty-one. He held the title for five years in a row."

Kalen was impressed. "No kidding? You were twenty-one when you won?" He glanced at the photo on the wall.

Dan smiled fondly at his photo. "Yeah, I used to be buff. Now I'm a working man. I've got the kids and the love handles to prove it," he said with a smile. He patted his rock-solid abs.

"As if!" Scott joked.

"How much is a membership?" Kalen asked.

"Sixty dollars a month. Your membership also includes a meeting with a personal trainer once a week for the first month. The trainer will help create a fitness program that's right for you," Dan replied.

Kalen hesitated. He knew he could afford up to thirty-five dollars a month. He was only working two days a week at the grocery store. He wanted to save a little bit of spending money. His parents would flip if he took more shifts at Howard's to pay for a gym membership. "Remember our agreement!" his mother had said.

There was a knock on the door. A big guy with a long black ponytail poked his head into the room. He wore a black t-shirt with "STAFF" across the chest in big letters.

"Dan? Do you have a minute? I want to show you something."

Dan nodded. "Sure, Jake." He turned to Scott and Kalen. "Listen, you think about it while I'm out. I'll be right back."

After Dan left the room, Scott turned to Kalen. "So have you made up your mind yet?"

Kalen frowned. "Well, it's more money than I planned to spend. It'll eat up most of my paycheck. I still need money for other stuff," Kalen said.

"It's a bit more cash, but you'll definitely see results," said Scott. "Dan will set you up with a fitness and nutrition plan. Before you know it, you'll be totally buff. It's worth it."

Kalen thought about what Scott said. If he needed more money, he could ask for another shift or two at work. *As long as my grades don't slip, my parents shouldn't mind,* he thought. Kalen decided to go for it.

Dan walked back into the room. "So? Have you made up your mind?"

"Sign me up!" Kalen said.

chapter 5

the new girl

The first day of school was a crisp, sunny day. The gymnasium of Bayview High was swarming with students. Everyone was getting their timetables and comparing classes. The new students were easy to pick out. They were the ones walking around in a daze. They clutched their timetables tightly and searched for their new homerooms.

Kalen scanned the crowd, looking for familiar faces. He saw his sister, Julia, standing with a group of grade nine girls. They were all carrying backpacks and looking very eager for class to begin. Kalen smiled. He remembered feeling a little excited in grade nine, too.

Kalen walked over to the "Grade Eleven, S to Z" table to pick up his timetable. A girl with a pierced eyebrow handed him his sheet. Kalen checked his classes and teachers.

"Agh, Watson the Warden for biology. Great," he muttered, scanning the page.

He felt a tap on his shoulder. "Excuse me, do you know where I could find Mr. Cooper's history classroom?" asked a voice behind him.

Kalen turned to see a tall, pretty girl with curly black hair standing behind him. She looked confused. Kalen saw that she was holding a timetable in her hand.

"Sure," Kalen said. "You go down this hall and turn left. Then take the stairs up to the top floor. Cooper's class is the first one on the right." He smiled. "You must be new at Bayview. My name is Kalen."

Her ringlets shook as she nodded. "I'm Anna. I just transferred from St. Mary's. It's my first year at a public high school. I used to wear a uniform at my old school. I had a hard time deciding what to wear today," she said. She tugged nervously at the hem of her denim skirt. She wore a purple turtleneck sweater that showed off her dark skin and eyes.

"What grade are you in this year?" Kalen asked her.

"Eleven," Anna replied. "You?"

"Same," Kalen answered.

"Do you play basketball?" Anna asked.

Kalen looked surprised. "Yeah. How did you know?"

"The shoes are a dead giveaway," Anna said with a smile, pointing at his feet. Kalen was wearing high-top court shoes.

"I play ball, too," Anna continued. "Maybe I'll see you on the court sometime."

"Hey, Kalen! Over here!"

Kalen looked over his shoulder. Scott and Amber were waving and walking toward him. Kalen waved back.

"I've got to jet. It was nice meeting you," Kalen said to Anna.

Anna smiled. "Sure. See you around."

Scott and Amber caught up with Kalen just as Anna was leaving. Scott was obviously checking her out.

"Who was *that?*" he asked.

Kalen shrugged. "A new girl. Anna. She was looking for Cooper's room. She said she plays basketball."

"She's pretty!" Scott said, staring at Anna as she walked away.

"What school is she from?" Amber interrupted. She gave Scott a dirty look.

"St. Mary's," Kalen said.

"The all-girls school?" Scott asked.

"Yeah, I think so," Kalen replied.

"Why didn't she stick around? You could've introduced us," Scott said, craning his neck to see where Anna had gone.

"Sorry, bud. I told her you were coming, and she took off. She has probably heard all about the Jansen charm from her friends at St. Mary's."

"Very funny, Sommers," Scott said. He gave Kalen a punch in the shoulder.

"Ow—hey, lay off, will you? There's a lot more power in that punch these days." Kalen rubbed his shoulder in mock pain.

"Yeah, you've really beefed up, Scott. Looking good," Amber said, looking him over.

Kalen glanced at Amber. Was she comparing him to Scott? He hoped not. Suddenly, Kalen felt self-conscious.

"We'd better get moving, or we'll be late for class," Kalen said. He leaned down and kissed Amber softly on the lips. "I'll meet you at your locker after school, okay?" he said.

"Okay. I may be a bit late. I want to talk to Madame Gaudette after school about taking advanced French this year," Amber replied. She checked her watch. "I'd better go. I don't want to be late for Cooper's class. See you later," she said. She squeezed Kalen's arm and headed off in the same direction as Anna.

"Did she say Cooper's class?" Scott asked. "She must be in that new girl's homeroom. Maybe Amber could make friends with her. She could put in a good word for me, maybe set us up?" Scott looked hopeful.

Kalen hauled his backpack onto his shoulder and shook his head. "Man, you're dreaming," he said. Then he pulled his timetable from his pocket. "First class—biology with Ms. Watson. Can't be late for that one—she locks the door as soon as the bell rings. Catch you later, Jansen," Kalen said, striding down the hall. He disappeared into the crowd of students.

Sitting in biology class, Kalen thought about Amber's reaction to Scott's new look. She had been totally impressed. More than ever, Kalen was determined to get in shape—and he was going to do it as fast as possible.

chapter 6

are you new here?

On Wednesday afternoon, Kalen walked into The Sweat Shop for his first workout. The warm air and sharp scent of sweat greeted him as he pushed open the glass doors.

Kalen walked up to the counter. He pulled out his membership card and waited in line to check in. The gym was really busy. He looked see through the glass wall. Almost every piece of equipment was being used. He checked his watch. It was almost four o'clock.

Where is Scott, he wondered. *He was supposed to meet me fifteen minutes ago. It isn't like him to be late.* Kalen glanced around. There was no sign of Dan, either. The woman behind the desk handed him a key for a locker. He took it and headed for the locker room.

Kalen changed into his workout gear. He decided to wait for Scott in the weight room. Without Scott, he felt like a total gym moron. The only things he had used were the dumbbells and barbells, which lay neatly stacked on racks against the walls. He didn't know how to use much of the bigger pieces of equipment.

Well, I can start with some hand weights, he thought. He stepped around a guy who was sitting on a bench. He was lifting a huge barbell over his head.

"Hey! What do you think you're doing?"

Kalen whipped around and saw the guy with the barbell glaring at him. "Just getting some weights," Kalen answered, confused. "Sorry—are you using these?"

"No," the guy snarled, "but I was lifting a lot of weight a minute ago. You got in my space. I could've dropped it on my head—or yours!"

"Okay, okay, I'm sorry," Kalen said.

The guy shot him another dirty look. He picked up his weights and moved to another bench nearby.

Kalen shook his head. *What a jerk*, he thought to himself.

"Hey, Kalen!"

Kalen turned at the sound of his name. It was Scott, walking quickly toward him.

"Dude! Sorry I'm late," Scott said. "Did you do anything yet?"

"Well, I just about got my head taken off by that guy over there," Kalen replied. He pointed at the barbell guy. "I guess I was in his way. Where were you?"

"I had to do something on the way here," Scott said. "Do you want to get started now?"

"Yeah. Let's pump some iron," Kalen said.

The boys sat down at a bench and began to warm up with some biceps curls. Kalen felt more comfortable as he moved from one area of the gym to the next. He was careful to watch where he was going. He made sure he didn't walk in front of anyone who was lifting heavy weights. If he did pass in front of someone, he said, "Excuse me" and got out of the way quickly.

Kalen had just finished one set of chest flys when a female voice asked, "Can I work in?" Kalen turned to see Anna, the new girl from school, standing behind him. She was wearing a purple tank top and a pair of black shorts. Her curly black hair was piled up on top of her head.

"You've got a bad habit of creeping up on people," Kalen said.

"Sorry," Anna said. "It's really busy in here, isn't it? Do you mind if I share the chest fly machine with you?"

"Not at all," Scott said, sticking out his hand. "Hi. I'm Scott."

"Scott, this is Anna," Kalen said. He could tell that Scott was dying to be introduced to her.

Anna smiled. "Hi, Scott."

"I didn't know you worked out here," Scott said as he moved his weights out of the way.

"I just joined this week. I used to go to another gym, but this place is closer to Bayview. It's easier for me to come here and work out right after basketball practice. Then I take the bus home from here. I live way across town," Anna answered.

"Where do you live?" asked Scott.

"Fairwell Street," Anna replied.

"Really? That's great—I live just around the corner," Scott said. "Maybe I could give you a ride home sometime. It beats taking the bus."

"Maybe," Anna said with a smile. She adjusted the weight on the machine and sat down to do chest flys.

Just then, Kalen saw the guy with the goatee enter the gym. Karl. His beady eyes darted around the room. Then he walked over to a big, muscular guy doing push-ups on a mat near the far wall. He began talking quietly to the guy doing push-ups. He looked around the gym as he spoke.

Scott looked over and saw the goatee guy. "I'll be back in a minute," he said over his shoulder. He walked toward Karl.

"Where are you going?" Kalen called, but Scott didn't hear him. Kalen shook his head. *So much for working out with Scott today,* he thought.

"So, have you been working out long?" Anna asked Kalen as they traded places.

Kalen positioned himself on the exercise machine and raised the weights. "No—first day today," he grunted as he lifted the weights above his head. His pectoral muscles were burning already.

"Scott is in pretty good shape, isn't he?" Anna observed.

Kalen grimaced as he finished his set. "Yeah. He used to be a lot smaller." Kalen frowned. "He probably wouldn't want me to tell you that."

Anna grinned. "I can keep a secret."

Scott came back. "Ready for power squats?" he asked Kalen.

"Sure," Kalen replied. "Hey, how do you know that guy?"

"What guy?" Scott asked, looking around.

"Karl. The guy you were just talking to!" Kalen said.

"Oh, him." Scott shrugged. "He just gives me tips once in a while, that's all. No big deal."

Anna picked up a set of free weights and turned to leave. "Thanks for the machine, guys," she said. "See you around."

Scott grinned at Anna. "Later." He watched her walk toward the locker room. "What a babe," he said to Kalen. "Do you think she'd go out with me?"

Kalen adjusted the weight on the squat machine. "I don't know. Ask her and find out."

"Easy for you to say, Sommers. You've got Amber. No pressure. A date every Saturday night. Me, I've got to work for it." Scott lowered the barbell across his shoulders and squatted. "This is too light." He stood up and added more weight.

Suddenly, they heard loud, angry voices from a corner of the room. *"Friggin' kids!* They need to learn some respect!"

Scott and Kalen turned in the direction of the yelling. Karl was shouting and pointing in their direction. Dan was standing next to him and speaking in a low voice.

Karl continued to yell. "There's no respect for the equipment, Dan! They just leave it lying around for other people to trip over. Do they think their mammas are going to come and pick up after them? You should set an age limit—no one under twenty-five allowed!"

Oh, man! thought Kalen. He'd forgotten to put away his dumbbells before he got on the chest fly machine. He'd just walked over to the squat machine and left them lying on the floor.

"This gym is for everyone, Karl. Even kids," Dan said firmly. "You need to calm down. You're bothering everyone."

Karl stormed off into the locker room. Dan started walking toward the two boys. He had serious look on his face. A muscle twitched in his jaw.

"Oh, *man.* Now we're going to get it," Kalen hissed to Scott.

"Boys. Come with me," Dan said.

chapter 7

'roid rage

Scott and Kalen sat across from Dan in his office. They could see through the glass wall that everyone had gone back to their workouts. Scott shifted in his seat. "Are we in trouble, Dan?" he asked.

Dan didn't say a word. From a counter behind his desk, he pulled out a hand blender and three plastic cups. He set them on his desk. There was a small fridge below the counter. Dan took out a banana, a carton of milk, and a tub of yogurt. He also took a jar of chocolate-flavored protein powder from a drawer in his desk. He mixed everything together to make three shakes. Dan set two of them in front of the boys.

"Cheers," he said. He downed his shake in one gulp.

Scott and Kalen looked at each other. They picked up their cups, drained them, and sat back waiting.

Dan looked through the glass wall and sighed heavily. "Some people take bodybuilding very, very seriously. I know I did when I was competing. There's a lot of pressure to be the biggest, hardest, and strongest. Some guys crack. Like Karl." Dan looked at Scott and Kalen. His face was serious. "What do you guys know about steroids?"

Kalen thought for a minute. "Um, they're illegal, right? And bodybuilders use them to get big fast."

"Yes," Dan said, "but do you know any of the side effects of using them?" He pulled a book down from a shelf behind his desk and read to them:

> Anabolic steroids are a group of powerful chemicals that are similar to the male sex hormone testosterone. Side effects in males include acne, stomach aches, nose bleeds, sleep problems, swollen breasts, and withered testicles.

Scott looked horrified. "Withered testicles?!" Dan looked up from the book. "Yeah. Your balls shrink." Scott looked disgusted. Dan continued to read.

Users may also have mood swings, depression, and anger.

Dan closed the book. "Or, as we call it in the bodybuilding industry, 'roid rage.

Kalen stared at Dan. "Are you saying that Karl is using steroids?"

Dan shrugged his huge shoulders, shaking his head. "Maybe. I don't know for sure. But the way he's been freaking out lately...I can't have that happening at my gym."

"What would you do if you found out someone here was using steroids?" Scott asked.

"If someone was using them at my gym or selling them to my members, I'd cancel their membership," said Dan. "I'm running a clean gym—no drugs." He stood up and threw the cups into the garbage. "Remember to pick up your weights when you're through using them. Put them back on the rack."

Kalen nodded. "Okay, no problem."

Later, as Kalen and Scott were showering, Kalen said, "Can you believe that Karl guy? He was having a 'roid rage right there in the gym!" He shook his head. "That's freaky."

Scott stepped out of the shower and grabbed his towel from a nearby hook. "Yeah. Freaky."

"Did you hear what Dan said about the side effects of steroids? Who wants muscles if your equipment might shrink?" Kalen said, shaking his head in disgust. He stuck his head under the spray of water and rubbed his face.

Scott frowned. "I know. That would *suck.*" He headed toward the lockers. "I'll meet you outside, all right?"

"Sure. I'll be right there." Kalen turned off the water and reached for his towel.

By the time Kalen reached the lockers, Scott was gone. Kalen pulled on his t-shirt and jeans and bent over to pull on his running shoes. Out of the corner of his eye, he noticed something small and yellow lying on the floor. He picked it up and examined it. It was some kind of pill.

Kalen turned the pill over and over in his hand. It could be anything, he figured. It could be for headaches, like aspirin. Or maybe Karl had dropped it. Maybe it was a steroid. Kalen paused, then stuffed the little yellow pill into his pocket. He would ask Dan about it next time he saw him.

chapter 8

mix it with what?

After the talk with Dan, Kalen decided to stay out of Karl's way. He didn't want to do anything to get Karl mad him and risk getting his head kicked in.

Kalen forgot about the yellow pill he'd found in the locker room. He was too absorbed in his diet and workouts. Within a couple of weeks, he had settled into his new routine:

9:00 –	3:30	School
3:30 –	4:30	Basketball practice
4:30 –	5:30	Work out
6:00 –	6:30	Dinner
6:30 –	7:00	Help clean up
7:00 –	9:00	Homework
9:00 –	10:00	TV & Talking to Amber
10:00		Bed

A few weeks after school started, Kalen made plans to meet up with Scott. The boys were going to The Sweat Shop to get some protein supplements. Dan had promised to help Kalen figure out what he needed to eat to bulk up. Kalen was working out regularly now. He was eager to start a diet to help him gain some weight and build some muscle.

Kalen grabbed his jacket and keys and headed for the door.

"Kalen, are you going to be working at Howard's tonight? I need some milk," Mrs. Sommers called.

"No, Mr. H. gave me the night off. I'm going out with Scott," he answered.

Mrs. Sommers met Kalen in the hall. "Well, stop at the store and pick up a carton of milk on your way home, please," she said. She put her hands on her hips and looked him over. "All this exercise must be good for you, Kalen. You are looking very fit and healthy these days." Any concerns his mother may have had about his workouts seemed to have disappeared.

"I told you not to worry about it, didn't I?" Kalen answered.

"Yes, but I'm your mother. It's my job to worry about my kids," she said firmly. "I have to admit, I was worried you may be taking on too much. You seem to be handling everything just fine, though. You also seem to be developing some muscle," his mother added with a smile.

Hearing her praise made Kalen feel good. "Thanks, Mom," he said, smiling back at her. She moved forward to hug him. "Ow—ooh, sore muscles," Kalen said, frowning. "Those shoulder presses were a killer."

He swung his backpack over one shoulder and winced. Ever since he'd started working out at The Sweat Shop, his muscles had been aching. Dan assured him that the pain wouldn't last long. He said that aching muscles were a good sign. It meant that the muscle tissue was repairing itself and growing stronger. Dan had explained that lifting weight caused tiny tears in the muscles. When Kalen was not working out, his body was healing those tears. That was why his body felt sore. Protein helped repair the muscles and make them grow larger.

It seemed to be true. Kalen was starting to see results. His biceps were more defined, and his neck and shoulders appeared wider.

He pulled on a baseball cap and picked up his gym bag. Outside, Scott beeped the horn and revved the engine. "I've got to go, Mom—see you later," Kalen said.

"Have fun!" Mrs. Sommers said as Kalen headed out the door.

The Sweat Shop was pretty quiet for a Friday night. Most of the members had already gone home. Kalen watched as a guy strutted by. He was holding his arms away from his sides and puffing out his chest. He seemed to be showing off his muscles.

"Look at that guy," Kalen whispered to Scott, nodding his head toward the strutting guy. "Do you see how he walks around like that? He must think he's Arnold Schwarzenegger! But this guy isn't even very big."

Scott nodded. "Yeah, I've seen him before. He's got ILS."

"What is ILS?"

"It stands for Imaginary Lat Syndrome. It's when guys walk around holding out their arms. They think the lat muscles under their arms are so big, they can't put their arms down at their sides!" Kalen and Scott laughed at the joke.

Kalen saw Dan in his glass office. He was talking to Jake, the personal trainer. Dan caught Kalen's eye and grinned. He waved the boys into his office.

Kalen and Scott looked at each other and shrugged. They made their way over to Dan's office to see what he wanted.

"Thanks for the update, Jake. Keep me informed if anything else comes up, okay?" Dan shook the big trainer's hand and walked him to the door of his office.

"Will do, boss," Jake replied. "Excuse me, guys," he said as he squeezed his wide shoulders past them and out the door.

"So!" Dan jumped up. "Let's get you set up with some protein supplements," he said to Kalen. "Follow me."

He led the boys to a storage room next to his office. Inside, Kalen saw shelves lining the walls. Bottles, jars, and boxes of all sizes were neatly stacked on each shelf. Kalen leaned up against a large plastic tub. He read the label. "CyberMaxx: For maximum muscle mass and weight gain. Recommended by champion bodybuilder Rico Romano, Mr. Ultimate 2001."

He looked up at Dan. "Does this stuff really work?" Kalen asked.

"It's important to do your research before you try any of these supplements, Kalen. What works for one person may not work for you. Take Jake, for example. He's been lifting weights for fifteen years. His body type is very different from someone like you, who is just starting to train. Your diet should be designed for *your* body's needs."

Dan took a small plastic jar from a higher shelf. "Since you're a teenager and your body isn't mature, I think you should try this one. It's a protein supplement to help you put on some weight. It will also repair your muscles after you work out. Drink two shakes every day, and you'll see results."

Kalen took the bottle and read the label. "Pro-Gain 2000," he read aloud. "Seven hundred calories per cup! Won't I get fat?" he asked, turning to Dan.

Dan shook his head. "No. You're going to be burning a lot of calories by working out. Your body will become better at processing the food you eat. It needs those calories to get enough nutrients," he said. "Drinking shakes doesn't mean you should stop eating real food, either. Keep eating foods like chicken, fish, fruits, and vegetables. Stay away from fad diets. You know, like that all-protein diet where people eat only meat and other types of protein. Your body does need protein. It also needs carbohydrates and fat. Yes, fat," he said firmly, seeing the doubtful look on Scott's face.

Kalen walked over to an open box filled with individually wrapped bars. "What about these?" he asked. "Are they for snacks, instead of chocolate bars or nachos?"

"Power bars are meant to be used as meal replacements. They're good for traveling because they don't need to be stored in a refrigerator. They're small and easy to carry. They also provide all the nutrients you need," Dan said. "Just don't replace *all* your meals with power bars."

"I keep a few bars in my gym bag in case I get hungry at school or practice," said Scott. "Some brands aren't too bad. But some taste like sweat socks."

By the time Kalen left the gym, he was loaded down with an extra-large tub of Pro-Gain 2000, a box of power bars, and a bag of skim milk powder. He'd also purchased a weight belt for weight training. It would help support his back when lifting heavy weights. He even bought a pair of gloves like the pros wear. Dan said the gloves would help him keep a solid grip on the metal bars when he was lifting. In total, he spent $150.00 at the gym. That did not even include the sixty dollars a month for his gym membership.

"Good thing I'm working," Kalen grumbled. He threw the bags into the back of Scott's Jeep. "I'm almost broke!"

"Yeah, but look at what you're getting!" Scott said, flexing his arms and shoulders.

chapter 9

liar!

By the middle of October, Kalen had been working out for six weeks. He could definitely see the results of his hard work. All the workouts and protein shakes had paid off.

Kalen's neck and shoulders filled out, and his arms were hard and muscular. Best of all, he had developed a six-pack of muscles on his stomach. He checked out his new ab muscles in the full-length mirror in his bedroom. He was pleased with the results of his exercise program. He wasn't quite as big as Scott yet. It would take more time and effort, he figured. *Pretty soon, I'll have the perfect body*, he thought.

Still, Kalen couldn't ignore the tiny fear that was growing in the back of his mind. His gym fees and supplements were expensive. He was getting very close to draining his bank account. He'd asked Mr. Howard for more hours at the grocery store, but he didn't want to work too much. If he did, his parents would start getting on his case about neglecting his homework. He was already spending most evenings at the gym. On top of it all, basketball season was almost finished. The semi-finals were coming up. Coach Nesbitt had planned extra practices to get ready for the Championship. Kalen was busier than ever.

One Tuesday night at the end of October, Kalen was sitting at the computer. He was doing his math homework. He stretched and yawned, rubbing his eyes. He glanced at the clock next to his bed. It was close to midnight. *Time to check my e-mail*, he thought.

Only three new messages. One was from Amber. Another was a joke from Scott. He read them both and then checked the third message. It was junk mail. He read the subject line.

GET A ROCK-SOLID BODY IN 2 WEEKS!!

Kalen started to hit the delete key and then paused. *How could anyone get a great body in two weeks*, he wondered. He had been working his butt off to get ripped, and it had taken him almost two months. Now Kalen was very curious. He clicked the message to open it.

It was an ad for anabolic steroids. Kalen remembered the talk he and Scott had earlier with Dan about this. The ad showed a photo of a guy with huge arms and legs and a ripped stomach.

Kalen read the words on the screen.

Kalen looked closely at the picture of the man on the screen. He couldn't see any of the side effects that Dan had mentioned. No acne or swollen breasts. *It wouldn't hurt to look at the website,* Kalen decided. He clicked on the link to Ana-Bulk's homepage.

Welcome to Ana-Bulk!
We sell only high-quality products.
Click on our Photo Gallery to see the
results for yourself!

Kalen scrolled down the screen. He saw links to the Photo Gallery, Products, Ordering Information, and Steroid Side Effects. He clicked on the link to read about the side effects. A long list appeared. The website explained the dangers.

Then, the website warned people against sharing needles. *Needles?* he thought. Kalen was surprised. He didn't know that steroids could be injected. He shuddered. *Why would anyone want to inject himself?* he thought.

He read on. The website also explained how to deal with many of the side effects. Other drugs were listed as useful treatments for many of them. *It seems stupid to take drugs to treat the side effects of other drugs*, Kalen thought.

As Kalen scrolled to the bottom of the page, he saw another warning. He noticed that very serious long-term side effects were in small print at the bottom of the page. Kalen read them aloud. He was surprised at how serious they were.

Taking steroids can cause liver
disease, cancer, and heart disease.

He shook his head in disbelief. *Steroids are way too dangerous*, he said to himself. Kalen could not understand why anyone would risk taking these drugs.

Farther down the page, there was a form for ordering steroids online. Kalen was shocked. He didn't know it was so easy to get steroids. It was just like ordering CDs on the Internet. Just click on the order number and type in a credit card number. The order would arrive in two weeks.

Kalen went back to the homepage. He clicked on the Photo Gallery. Photos began appearing on the page. The pictures showed men and women posing in tiny swimsuits. Their bodies were tanned and shining. They grinned as they flexed for the camera. Their bodies were huge and muscular. Kalen could hardly believe the size of their muscles. It looked impossible!

Kalen kept looking through the pictures. He stopped at a photo of a ripped guy who looked about twenty-five years old. The wide smile and cropped blond hair looked familiar to Kalen. Then Kalen's mouth fell open. It was Dan from The Sweat Shop!

The words under Dan's photo were "Danny Moller, Mr. Ultimate 1991 to 1996. Danny credits his amazing body to one of Ana-Bulk's most popular products, Decabolan-500."

Dan uses steroids, Kalen thought. Kalen felt sick. He had trusted Dan and followed his advice.

Kalen logged off and turned off the computer. He sat staring at the black screen for a long time. He was angry at Dan for pretending to be a friend and for lying about the steroids. Mostly Kalen was angry with himself. He felt like an idiot. It seemed that no matter how long he exercised, he would never look like the guys in the magazines. Not without steroids.

He turned off the light and got into bed, but he couldn't sleep. He lay awake, staring into the darkness of his room. He tried to sort out all the confusing thoughts in his head.

chapter 10

food fight

"**Y**eah, I know he used 'roids. All the top bodybuilders do."

Kalen stared at Scott. The two boys were sitting in the cafeteria at school, eating lunch. Kalen had just told Scott what he found on the Internet the night before. He told him about the effects of steroids. He also told him about Dan. Scott didn't look surprised. Now he was saying that he knew all along that Dan was on the juice.

"And you're not mad?" Kalen asked.

"No, why should I be? It's his body, so it's his decision," Scott answered, taking a bite of his sandwich.

"Dan said he'd kick out anyone who used them at The Sweat Shop! How can he say that when he is using them *himself!*"

"Calm down, okay?" Scott said, looking around. "You're making a scene."

Kalen sat back in his chair, shaking his head. He couldn't figure out Scott. Kalen had expected him to be surprised about Dan.

"I guess I just feel ripped off, that's all," Kalen said. "Dan talks about fitness and health, but he doesn't practice what he preaches."

Scott shrugged. "Don't worry about it. He set you up on a program, and it's working, right? He's not forcing *you* to take 'roids."

Kalen sighed heavily. "Yeah, I guess you're right. It doesn't matter." The cafeteria door opened and Amber walked in with some friends. She looked around the room and caught Kalen's eye. She smiled at him and waved. She said something to one of her friends and headed in his direction.

"Hi, babe," she said, leaning down to kiss Kalen. "Hey, Scott."

"Hey," Scott said. He shoveled pasta salad into his mouth.

Amber perched on Kalen's knee and put an arm around his neck. "Guess what's playing at the Cineplex this weekend? *Jurassic Park Four!* Do you want to go see it?" she asked.

"Um, I'm kind of strapped for cash this week, Amber. Can we go next weekend?" Kalen asked.

"Well, I could pay for the movie this weekend. Even though it's *your* turn!" Amber teased him.

Kalen gave her a squeeze. "That would be great. I'll pay next time, I promise. So, are you coming to my basketball game tomorrow night?" he asked. "I think my sister Julia wants to go, too."

Amber nodded. "Yeah, I'll pick her up around six-thirty tonight. It's the semi-finals, right?" she asked.

"Yeah. We're pumped to win," Kalen said, grinning. "We're in first place, and we're going to stay there, right Jansen?"

Scott wiped his mouth on a paper napkin and burped loudly. "Yeah—oh, sorry Amber," he said.

She gave him a disgusted look, and he laughed. Amber rolled her eyes. "I have history class after lunch. I'll make sure I tell Anna about your perfect table manners," she said.

Scott leaned forward and put one massive arm on the table. He flexed his biceps to make the muscle jump out. "One look at these pipes and Anna will forget about my table manners," he said proudly.

"You guys think it's all about muscles, don't you?" Amber said. "It doesn't matter how big you are if you still act like a pig," she said. "Or if you're cheap," she said with a smile, poking Kalen in the arm.

Kalen smiled. "Point taken," he said.

"Hey, speaking of Anna…there she is," Amber said. Amber pointed toward the cafeteria doors.

"Where?" asked Scott, looking around.

"Over there in the hallway," said Amber. She squinted, trying to see better. "Uh-oh. She's talking to that loser, Seth."

Anna walked into the cafeteria and stood in line. She seemed to be trying to ignore Seth, who followed her to the end of the line. He was obviously putting the moves on her.

Scott stood up. "I'm still hungry," he announced. "I think I'll get some yogurt."

"What, no potato chips? No ice cream bar?" Amber teased.

Scott made a face. "No way. They're *way* full of fat."

Amber rolled her eyes. "Whatever. You just want to talk to Anna. It drives you crazy that she's talking to Seth."

"As if!" Scott said. But he was smiling as he walked toward the food line.

Kalen frowned. "I hope he doesn't start something stupid with that guy."

"He won't," Amber said. "Scott's not the type of guy to go around picking fights."

They watched Scott stroll over to Anna and Seth. Seth glared at Scott and said something. Scott's face turned red, and he said something back. He was angry. Anna looked annoyed. She walked away from the boys, who were glaring at each other.

"What's going on?" asked Amber, stretching her neck to see them.

"I don't know," said Kalen. "But it looks bad."

Suddenly, they heard a loud *SPLAT!* A plate of fries with gravy landed on the wall next to their table. Gravy oozed down the wall and formed a puddle on the floor. A couple of girls screamed nearby.

"What the heck…" Kalen said, confused.

Amber wiped splatters of gravy from her arms. "Gross!" she said in disgust.

"FOOD FIGHT!" shouted a voice. Students were shouting and shrieking. Food began flying around the cafeteria. Some people started running for the door, but they were attacked with sandwiches, chicken burgers, and more fries. Russ Daniels and Matt Webb were standing on a table at the back of the cafeteria. They were gleefully throwing handfuls of tuna casserole and strawberry Jell-O.

"Oh, crap," muttered Kalen. He grabbed Amber's hand and pulled her out of her chair. "Duck!" he yelled.

Kalen and Amber dove under the table just in time. A plastic tub of spaghetti leftovers flew over the table.

"Where is Scott?" Kalen asked. He tried to look around without getting food in his face. Tomato sauce dripped over the edge of the table and onto the floor. Amber cringed. "Ugh. Let's get out of here," she said.

The teachers began shouting and trying to get control. Mr. Cooper and Coach Nesbitt started pulling the pranksters out of the mess. Mr. Cooper hauled Russ Daniels and Matt Webb down to the office. They were covered in food and were laughing.

"Come on!" Kalen and Amber ran toward the door. Students were standing around wiping food stains off their clothes. Kalen looked around for Scott, but he was nowhere to be seen. "I'm going to wash my hands," said Amber. She was sticky with gravy.

Kalen leaned closer. "What's in your hair?" he asked, reaching out to touch it. "Gravy," he said. He tried not to smile.

"What!? Oh, no," moaned Amber as she ran toward the girls' bathroom.

A few minutes later, Scott appeared. There wasn't a speck of food on him. "Hey, man, did you get bombed?" he asked, grinning.

Kalen shook his head. "Not really. Amber got a gravy shower, but that's all. Looks like you got out clean," he observed.

Scott nodded. "Yeah. But I hardly got to say two words to Anna. Seth was butting in," he said, frowning.

Kalen looked amused. "Weren't *you* the one who went over there because you saw him talking to her?" he asked.

Scott shrugged. "Maybe."

"Well, at least you didn't get chocolate pudding in the face while you were talking," said Kalen. He pointed at a girl who was trying to comb pudding from her long, curly hair without success.

Scott grinned. "Yeah."

Amber walked out of the bathroom. "Is it all gone?" she asked anxiously, turning this way and that.

Kalen put an arm around her. "Yes," he said, kissing the top of her head. He sniffed. "Mmm, you smell tasty," he said, grinning.

Amber made a face. "Thanks."

chapter 11

zits

On Thursday night, the gym at Bayview High was packed with students. The semi-final game was in the final quarter. A hush fell over the crowd that filled the bleachers.

Kalen stepped up to take a foul shot. Sweat rolled down his forehead, stinging his eyes. He bounced the ball three times for good luck and glanced up at the scoreboard. The game was tied, 42-42. With only eighteen seconds left on the clock, the Bayview Sharks needed Kalen to make this shot to win the game. He took a deep breath and focused on the net. He raised the ball, took aim, and let it fly through the air...

...SWISH!

The crowd erupted in a thunderous cheer, stomping their feet and clapping. The second shot followed the first one through the net. Within seconds, the game was over. The Sharks had won! Kalen's teammates crowded around to slap him on the back. A hand grabbed his shoulder. He turned around to see Coach Nesbitt beaming at him.

"Great play, Sommers! Looks like we're going to make it to the Championship!" the Coach shouted.

"Thanks, Coach!" Kalen replied, trying to catch his breath.

"Kalen! Over here!"

Kalen turned away from the coach and saw Amber standing up on the bleachers. His sister, Julia, stood next to her. They were waving madly to get his attention.

Coach Nesbitt smiled and slapped him on the back. "Get out of here, Sommers," he said. "Don't forget—practice is at four o'clock tomorrow afternoon!"

Kalen grinned. "Okay, Coach. See you later," he called over his shoulder. He squeezed through the crowd of people in the gymnasium and jogged toward the girls.

"That was amazing, Kalen! Great shot," Amber said, smiling up at him.

"Yeah, we rocked," Kalen agreed happily. "We couldn't have done it without Scott. He played a great third quarter. Did you see him slam three baskets in a row? He was on *fire!*"

"Let's talk about the game over a burger at Lee's," cut in Julia. "I'm starving!"

Kalen smiled at his little sister. "All right, Jules. Let's get out of here," he said. He slung one sweaty arm around her shoulders.

"Ugh, Kalen, you're totally sweaty. We'll meet you outside—*after* you shower," Julia said, disgusted. She pulled away from him.

Kalen laughed and pulled his arm away. He pretended to be offended. "Okay, I can take a hint. See you in a minute," he said, messing up Julia's blond curls. He gave Amber a quick kiss and headed for the locker room.

The locker room echoed with the triumphant shouts of the Bayview Sharks.

"Man, we kicked butt tonight! One more game and the Cup's coming home!" Kalen said as he and Scott came out of the showers.

"Yeah, what a game!" Scott said, wrapping a towel around his waist. Another towel hung over his head and shoulders. "I was so pumped in the second half. I didn't miss a shot," he said, grinning from ear to ear.

"If we keep playing like we did today, we'll win the Cup for sure," Kalen said. He searched in his gym bag, tossing his dirty clothes on the floor. "Hey, man, have you got any deodorant? I forgot my stick."

"Sure, just a minute," Scott said. He reached up to grab the deodorant from the top shelf of his locker. As he did, the towel around his shoulders fell off and landed on the floor.

Kalen looked at Scott in amazement. His entire back was covered in large, red pimples. Acne had spread across his shoulders. It covered his back right down to the towel wrapped around his waist. It looked like an angry, red rash. Kalen looked down at the floor so Scott wouldn't see him staring.

Scott quickly turned around and tossed the deodorant at Kalen.

"Catch," he said and pulled a clean t-shirt over his head. "I think I've got a rash from that new soap they're putting in the showers," he said. "My back is breaking out."

"It's not that bad," Kalen said. He swiped the deodorant under his arms and gave it back to Scott. "Thanks," he said.

"No problem," Scott said. He zipped up his gym bag and swung it over one shoulder. "Are you ready?"

"Yeah, just a minute," Kalen replied. He quickly tied his shoes and then followed Scott out the door.

chapter 12

a bad taste
in my mouth

Lee's Restaurant was packed with students when Kalen, Scott, Amber, and Julia arrived. It was a popular hangout. Lee's was always busy after basketball games.

The place didn't look like anything special. Mr. Lee, the owner, hadn't replaced the worn floor tiles in years. The wooden booths were scarred and dented. Everyone kept coming to Lee's because Mr. Lee made the best hamburgers and onion rings in town. Plus, he didn't seem to mind if the place was packed with kids. Mr. Lee knew they were his best customers.

Amber spotted a small booth in the corner. The four of them squeezed in. They talked and laughed loudly while they waited for the waitress. She came over carrying a tray full of drinks and a stack of menus. She tossed the menus onto the table and kept walking. She called over her shoulder, "I'll be right back to take your order," she said. She headed toward a crowded table to deliver the drinks.

"Man, I'm hungry," Kalen said, scanning the menu. "I could eat two of everything. What are you having, Amber?"

"I think I'll have onion rings and a diet soda," Amber said. She closed her menu. She reached for Kalen's hand under the table and leaned closer to him. "I'm glad we're out together tonight, Kalen," she said quietly. She didn't want Scott and Julia to hear her. "You've been so busy lately. I feel like we've hardly seen each other."

Kalen squeezed Amber's hand. "I know. I'm sorry. I'm just...busy," he said. He tried to smile.

Kalen was excited about the win, but he was also really tired. All he wanted to do was eat and go home to bed. He had a French test tomorrow, and he still needed to study. Plus, he had basketball practice tomorrow after school. After that, he had to work at Howard's until ten o'clock. He still hadn't figured out how he was going to squeeze a workout into his busy day. Now Amber was complaining that they didn't see enough of each other.

"We'll do something together this weekend. I promise," Kalen said. "I don't have any plans for Saturday afternoon. I get off work at one o'clock. Why don't we go for an ice cream cone on the boardwalk?"

Amber shook her head. "I can't. I have plans to go out with Kim and Lisa. Are you free on Sunday afternoon?"

Kalen frowned. "That's when I work out. I also picked up an extra shift at work on Sunday night. I guess Sunday is out, too."

Amber pulled her hand away. "Well, I guess we won't be doing anything together this weekend," she said. Her voice sounded cold.

"I can't help it, Amber! I have to stick to my schedule, or I won't get any bigger. I have to work to pay for the supplements. Not to mention my gym membership." Kalen stopped suddenly. He realized he was raising his voice.

Amber looked mad. Scott and Julia were sitting quietly next to them. They were looking down at the scratched tabletop.

The waitress returned to take their orders. "What'll it be, kids?" she asked.

Julia spoke first. "I'll have an order of onion rings and a large orange soda."

"What about you, hon? What are you having?" the waitress asked Amber.

"I'm not really hungry," Amber said, shooting a dark look at Kalen. "I'll just have a strawberry milkshake."

"You can share my onion rings," Julia said.

"Thanks, Julia," Amber said, trying to smile.

"And what will you guys have?" said the waitress, turning to Kalen and Scott.

"I'll have two grilled chicken sandwiches. Hold the buns and the mayonnaise, please. I want a green salad instead of fries and light Italian dressing on the side," said Scott. He handed the waitress his menu.

The waitress raised an eyebrow at him. "You want sandwiches with no buns?"

"Yes," said Scott.

"Okey-dokey," said the waitress. "And you?" she said, looking at Kalen.

Kalen thought for a minute. "I'll have the same," he said.

After the waitress left, Julia leaned across the table at her brother. "What kind of order is that?" she asked. "You always get a double cheeseburger with fries and gravy."

"I haven't eaten that stuff in months," Kalen replied, looking annoyed. "It's too greasy. I need to watch my diet. I can't just eat junk anymore. I've got to feed the machine!" He patted his chest and flexed one arm.

Julia rolled her eyes. Amber just ignored him and stared out the window.

"It's true," said Scott. "You can't expect to get ripped if you eat junk food."

Suddenly, Scott noticed Anna sitting at a nearby table with a group of students. "Hey, there's Anna. She looks *great*," he said. Her long black curls fell over the shoulders of her soft white sweater.

Julia giggled. "Scott, why don't you just ask her out, for Pete's sake?"

"I think she'd go out with you Scott," Amber added. "I overheard her talking to Tracy Wong in history. She said she thinks you're cute."

Scott's eyes widened. "She did?"

"Yeah." He glanced over at Anna's table. She was talking to the girl sitting next to her. They were laughing about something.

He took a deep breath. "Okay, here goes," Scott said. He began walking toward Anna's table. He had a determined look on his face.

"Did she really say that?" Julia whispered.

"I don't know for sure, but Scott needed a little push," Amber replied, grinning.

Suddenly, Seth Morgan sauntered into the restaurant with Russ and Matt. He looked around for an empty table, but there were none. His dark eyes settled on Kalen.

chapter 13

out of control

"**H**ey, Sommers, are you finished eating yet?" he asked. Seth walked over and leaned on Kalen's table.

"We haven't even started," Kalen answered.

"Well, in that case, we'll just have to join you," said Seth. He and his friends sat down and pushed Julia and Amber over. They squashed the girls over to one side of the restaurant booth.

"Hey! Get off me, you loser!" Julia yelled, pushing back at them.

Kalen stood up. He grabbed Seth by the shoulder and yanked him out of the booth.

"Why don't you try pushing *me*, butthead?" Kalen said. Now, he was standing nose to nose with Seth.

"No problem," Seth snarled. He shoved Kalen and nearly knocked him over. Some kids nearby turned their heads in Kalen and Seth's direction. People were beginning to gather around to see what was going on.

"Hey! What's going on?" a voice yelled. It was Scott. He pushed through the crowd and walked up to Seth. "Have you got a problem, Morgan?" Scott said.

"Yeah. You're my problem, Jansen," Seth growled at him.

"Well, let's take it outside and solve it!" Scott shot back.

"FIGHT!" shouted someone in the crowd.

Kalen and Scott went outside to the parking lot behind Lee's Restaurant. Seth, Russ, and Matt followed them. All the students ran outside to watch.

"Kalen! Stop it! This is stupid," Amber said, following Kalen out to the parking lot. Julia ran after them. She had a scared look on her face.

"What am I supposed to do, Amber? Let Scott fight these idiots by himself?" Kalen said. He sounded impatient. "Just hang back with Julia, all right?" He walked away. Amber and Julia stood there looking worried.

"Come on, Julia," Amber said. She pulled Julia back into Lee's.

The crowd formed a circle around the boys. Scott and Kalen stood facing Seth, Matt, and Russ. They each waited for the other to make the first move.

"Come on, Morgan! Take your best shot," Scott yelled.

"What's the matter, Sommers? Are you afraid your little sister will tell your mamma?" sneered Seth.

"Shut your mouth," Kalen said angrily. He was itching to punch Seth right in the face. He had enough of this guy already.

Suddenly, Seth lunged at Scott. The two boys fell to the ground, rolling and wrestling with each other. Seth got in two or three hard punches to Scott's stomach. Then Scott jerked his body to one side, throwing Seth off him. He jumped on Seth and began punching him in the face. Seth kept trying to get out from under Scott, but Scott was too heavy. Scott had him pinned to the ground.

Kalen saw Russ run over to help Seth. He slammed into Russ from behind, and they fell onto the pavement. Russ lay there, gasping for breath. Kalen had knocked the wind out of him.

Kalen looked up. Scott was really laying into Seth. Kalen heard a sickening crunch as Scott pounded Seth's face with his fists. Blood gushed from Seth's nose, and he tried to cover his face with his hands. Scott's face was twisted with rage. Kalen had never seen him out of control before. He didn't think Scott would stop until Seth was dead.

Kalen left Russ lying on the pavement and ran over to Scott and Seth. Kalen grabbed Scott's shoulders and tried to pull him off, but it was like trying to stop a train. Scott slammed his fists into Seth's ribs, and Seth howled in pain.

"Scott! Get off him! It's over," Kalen yelled, pulling as hard as he could.

Finally, Scott let go of Seth and fell back. He was breathing heavily. His cheek was cut and bleeding, and his knuckles were raw. Seth lay on the ground, groaning. Russ and Matt ran over to help him up, but he screamed with pain when he tried to move.

A police siren wailed, getting closer every second. The crowd scattered in all directions. Amber and Julia came running out of Lee's with Mr. Lee behind them. The next thing Kalen knew, he and Scott were hauled to their feet. A police officer began questioning them.

"What's going on here? Who started this fight?" one of the officers asked.

"He did, sir," Kalen answered, pointing at Seth. A police officer was bending over Seth and checking his injuries. Seth was almost out cold. Both of his eyes were beginning to turn purple. His nose was bent badly.

"He's really beaten up. His nose looks broken, and I think he may have a cracked rib or two. We'd better call an ambulance," said the police officer.

"I called already," Mr. Lee said.

"Good." The first officer turned back to Kalen and Scott. "You boys are coming with me. We'll need to talk to your parents."

Kalen was filled with fear. His parents would freak when they found out he had been fighting.

chapter 14

sorry about your face

When the ambulance arrived, the emergency team loaded Seth onto a stretcher. Kalen, Amber, Julia, and Scott got into the squad car. They sat silently. They were too afraid to speak. Scott stared out the window until they arrived at 16 Cherrytree Street.

Inside the Sommers' house, the police officer explained the situation to Kalen's parents. Mrs. Sommers saw the blood on Kalen's jacket and went pale. "Are you all right?" she asked.

"Yeah, Mom. I'm fine," Kalen answered.

"Unfortunately, the other boy looks far worse than these two," the officer said sternly. "His family may wish to press charges. If I need any more information, I'll be in touch." He got up to leave.

"Thank you for bringing them home, Officer. If we can help in any way, please let us know," Mr. Sommers said. He walked the police officer to the door.

When he returned to the living room, he fixed a stern eye on Kalen and Scott. "I'm going to call Scott's parents and tell them to come and pick up Scott. We'll explain the situation when they get here. They can take Amber home, too." He left the room.

"Are you okay?" Mrs. Sommers asked Julia.

Julia nodded. Her lips were trembling. Then she burst into tears. Mrs. Sommers put her arms around her and patted her back. "Shhh, it's okay. It's going to be fine," she said as Julia sobbed on her shoulder. Mrs. Sommers glared at Kalen over Julia's shoulder. Kalen looked down at his shoes. He knew he was in for it.

Once Julia had calmed down, Mrs. Sommers sent her upstairs to bed. Mr. Sommers came back into the room.

"Mr. Jansen is on his way to pick up Scott." He crossed his arms and stared at Kalen and Scott.

"Amber, do you need anything? A glass of milk?" Mrs. Sommers asked, putting an arm around Amber's shoulders.

Amber shook her head. "No thanks, Mrs. Sommers," she said quietly. Her face was pale.

Kalen saw the look on Amber's face, and he felt terrible. He should have just walked away from Seth in the parking lot. He couldn't just let Scott fight those guys alone, though. It never should have gotten so bad. He felt sick remembering the sight of Scott's fist slamming into Seth's bloody face, over and over again. Scott had been out of control. Now, Scott was sitting quietly on the couch. He was just staring at his hands in his lap.

The doorbell rang, and Mr. Sommers went to answer the door. Kalen heard him speaking in a low voice to Scott's father.

Mr. Jansen came into the living room and said, "Let's go, Scott. Your mother is waiting in the car." He turned to Amber and said, "We'll take you home now, Amber. Your grandmother is waiting for you." Amber nodded and stood up.

Slowly, Scott stood up. He avoided looking at Mr. and Mrs. Sommers. "I'm sorry about all this. It's all my fault. Kalen didn't want to fight anyone." He glanced at Kalen. "Sorry, man." He followed his father out the door.

Kalen walked Amber to the door. "Amber..." he said helplessly.

She shook her head. "Forget it, Kalen. I'm too tired to talk now. Call me tomorrow, okay?" Amber walked out.

Kalen walked back to the living room. He knew his parents were going to punish him. His mother and father were sitting on the couch waiting for him. Kalen sat in the chair across from them and waited for the shouting to start.

"Kalen." Mrs. Sommers' voice was heavy with disappointment. "It's not like you or Scott to be fighting. What happened?"

Kalen told his parents how Seth had started the fight. He also told them that Scott had really lost his temper. "I've never seen him so mad," Kalen said, shaking his head in disbelief. "It wasn't that he *wouldn't* stop hitting Seth, it was like he *couldn't* stop."

Mr. Sommers sighed. "Well, Scott had better hope that the other boy's parents don't press charges. Scott could be in a lot of trouble."

"You'd better let Scott and his parents worry about that," Mrs. Sommers said sternly, looking at Kalen. "You have enough to worry about. Like your punishment for fighting."

Here it comes, Kalen thought. Grounded. No car. No phone...

"No workouts for two weeks," Mrs. Sommers said firmly.

"What! Mom, you can't do that," Kalen said. "I'll lose all my muscle! It's taken me months to look like this."

"No arguments, Kalen. You will go to school and basketball practice, and then you'll come straight home. You will work at Howard's only on the weekend. No dates. Maybe next time you'll think twice before you get into a fight," his mother said. "Now go upstairs to bed. It's past eleven o'clock."

"Fine," he said angrily. Kalen grabbed his gym bag and went upstairs.

Kalen lay in bed. He thought about everything that happened. The day started out great. The game had been so awesome, but then he'd had that fight with Amber. She'd been mad about spending so little time together lately. Now he wouldn't be able to see her at all for two whole weeks.

Great, he thought, *just great.* And no workouts, either. He fought the panicky feeling in his stomach. He'd worked so hard to bulk up, and now he was going to lose it because of a stupid fight. It wasn't even his fault!

Maybe I could work out at home, he thought. His dad had some old weights in the garage. As Kalen drifted off to sleep, he wondered what happened to Scott when he got home.

chapter 15

no more chances

On Friday morning, Kalen waited at Amber's locker after second period. He knew she had a spare, and he wanted to talk to her about the night before.

Seth was at school on Friday, too. His nose was broken, and his eyes were bruised and puffy. He was walking very carefully. Apparently, he had a cracked rib. Everyone at school had either seen the fight or heard about it. Kalen hadn't talked to Scott yet. He hoped that Seth hadn't decided to press charges against Scott.

Amber came around the corner with a group of girls. They were laughing. When she saw Kalen leaning against her locker, the smile faded from her lips. Her friends whispered among themselves. Amber said, "I'll catch up with you later." The girls walked past Kalen without looking at him.

Amber walked up to Kalen and began fiddling with the lock on her locker. "Hi," she said, avoiding his eyes.

"Hi," he said. He leaned down to kiss her, but she turned her face away. She unloaded her books into her locker and slammed the door.

"What's the matter?" Kalen asked. Amber looked away and said nothing to him. "Can we talk about last night?" he asked, trying to catch her attention.

Amber looked Kalen straight in the eye. "What do you want to talk about?"

"Look, I'm sorry I was such a jerk. I shouldn't have gotten involved, but what was I supposed to do? Let Scott get beaten up?"

"He looked like he could handle himself," Amber replied in a cold voice.

Kalen sighed. "Yeah, I guess he did," he said.

"Is there something else you want to tell me, Kalen? Because I have to go to the library and study," Amber said.

Kalen bit his lip. "Yeah, I just wanted to let you know I...I'm kind of grounded for the next two weeks...so, um, that ice cream cone..."

Amber sighed and shook her head. "I knew it," she said. "I knew you'd get grounded. It doesn't matter, Kalen. I've been thinking. Maybe we should take a break."

Kalen frowned. "A break? What do you mean by that?"

Amber looked down at the floor. "I mean, we hardly ever see each other, and…you're so different now, Kalen. Ever since you started working out. You don't seem to have time for me. You're always at the gym or working at the grocery store."

"That's not true!" Kalen exploded.

"All your time and money goes into your gym membership and your protein powders…" Amber looked up at Kalen. Her brown eyes filled with tears. "I think we should break up."

Kalen felt like he'd been punched in the stomach. He hadn't expected this. He just stared at Amber. She looked away.

"Fine," Kalen said in a hurt voice. "I guess I'll see you around." He turned and walked away from her.

Kalen went into the nearest washroom and threw his backpack on the floor. He went into a stall and slammed the door, cursing. He leaned against the stall door and took a deep breath. He tried to pull himself together. Things were getting worse and worse. His eyes stung, and he rubbed them with the back of his hand.

The washroom door opened. Kalen heard footsteps and then the sound of running water. The water stopped. Then Kalen heard the beeping of a cell phone. He listened.

"Yeah. It's me. Scott."

Kalen listened, surprised. Scott?

"I'll be there after school. Listen, I've hit a plateau. I need some new gear. No darts. Can you get it? Great. Bye." The phone beeped as Scott turned it off.

Kalen heard the washroom door swing shut as Scott left. *What was that all about?* he wondered. *Who was Scott talking to?*

Kalen unlocked the stall door. He tried to sort out the thoughts and feelings swirling around in his mind. It was too confusing. He didn't want to think about any of it. Throwing his backpack over his shoulder, he went off to class.

Time ticked by slowly. The hands on the clock in Kalen's biology class seemed to stand still. He thought the day would never end. Finally the bell rang, and everyone packed up their books to go home. Kalen breathed a sigh of relief. *I'm glad this day is over,* he thought.

Outside, Kalen looked around for Scott. He saw Julia standing with her friends. She caught his eye and walked over to him.

"Hi," she said.

"Hi, Jules," Kalen said, smiling at his sister. "Are you okay?"

"Yeah, I'm fine," she replied, smiling back. "Last night was just...weird."

"I know. Have you seen Scott?" he asked.

Julia shook her head. "No. I saw Amber though. She was crying in the girls' bathroom on the third floor. She said you two broke up."

Kalen looked at the ground. "Yeah, we did."

"That sucks," Julia said sadly. "I really like Amber," she added.

"Me too," Kalen said, sighing heavily. Then he saw Scott coming out of the school. "I'll see you at home, okay?" he said to his sister.

"Okay," said Julia.

"Scott!" Kalen hollered. "Wait up!"

Scott turned around. As Kalen walked closer, he could see that Scott had a black eye. The cut on his cheek looked red and sore.

"Nice face," Kalen said with a smile.

"Thanks," Scott answered.

"Hey, what happened when you got home last night?" Kalen asked.

Scott frowned. "Well, my parents freaked out when I told them Seth probably had a broken nose and ribs. They were worried Seth would press charges against me or something. Vice-principal MacDougall called me into her office today to talk about the fight. Seth and his parents were there, too. So was Coach Nesbitt."

"What happened?"

"Seth admitted that he started the fight. He doesn't want to press charges. But Coach benched me for the rest of the season. I won't be playing in the Championship game," Scott explained.

"What!? Oh no. Are you serious? We need you on the team. We're so dead," Kalen groaned.

"Well, I'm just glad Seth isn't pressing charges against me. I can deal with the suspension from the team," said Scott.

They reached Scott's Jeep. Scott unlocked the doors and tossed his backpack into the backseat. "Are you going to the gym?"

Kalen shook his head. "Nope. My parents grounded me for two weeks. No gym, no dates—nothing," he said gloomily. "So much for my abs."

Scott shrugged. "I wouldn't worry about it. Two weeks is no big deal. You can do some exercises at home. Try doing some push-ups and ab crunches."

Just then, Anna walked by with a group of girls. Scott smiled and waved. She stared at him with an icy look on her face and then looked away. Scott's face fell.

"Perfect. She thinks I'm a jerk. Now I'll never get a chance with her," he said angrily. He kicked at a soda can on the ground.

"Maybe she's been talking to Amber," Kalen grumbled. "She dumped me today."

Scott didn't seem to hear him. "I suppose Anna thinks she's *all that*. Well, plenty of other girls will go out with me. What's her problem, anyway?" he wondered out loud.

Kalen glanced at Scott. "She probably thinks you're crazy after the way you beat up Seth. What got into you, anyway? It's not like you to freak out like that."

Scott whipped around and snarled, "What are you talking about?"

Kalen was surprised by the angry look on Scott's face.

"Well," Kalen went on, "I've known you since we were kids. I've never seen you lose it like that. I mean, you busted Seth's nose, Scott! And you kept on hitting him, even though he was begging you to stop."

Scott narrowed his eyes at Kalen. "Thanks a lot, Kalen. Of all my friends, I figured *you'd* back me up. I guess I was wrong." He turned to leave.

"Scott, remember I *did* back you up," said Kalen angrily.

Scott ignored him. He started to leave.

"Wait!" Kalen took a deep breath. He had been thinking about Scott's strange behavior all afternoon. "I overheard you talking on your cell phone today in the bathroom. You know, after second period."

"So?" Scott turned back to look at Kalen.

"So, you said something about a 'plateau' and 'darts.' What was all that about? Who were you talking to?" Kalen asked.

Scott's face turned red. "You've been *spying* on me?"

"No! I just happened to be in the washroom too. You left before I could say anything. Who were you talking to?" Kalen repeated.

"It's none of your business!" Scott snapped. He turned to get into his jeep but Kalen grabbed his arm. Scott turned back. He took a swing at Kalen, barely missing his jaw. Kalen stepped back in surprise.

For a moment, the two boys stood frozen. They stared at each other in shock. Then Scott jumped into the jeep and roared out of the parking lot. He left Kalen standing there with his mouth open.

chapter 16

the real deal

Since Kalen had lost his right to drive the car for two weeks, he walked ten blocks to the gym. He had to find Scott. He knew his mother would kill him when he got home, but he needed to deal with Scott right away. It was four-thirty when Kalen arrived at The Sweat Shop.

He couldn't believe Scott had tried to hit him. What was his problem? Who had Scott been talking to on the phone? Kalen was so deep in thought that he didn't notice Dan until he ran into him.

"Whoa! Kalen! Are you in a hurry?" Dan asked, smiling.

Kalen stared angrily at Dan. "Excuse me. I'm looking for Scott." He pushed past Dan and started walking toward the locker room.

Dan stopped smiling. "Kalen, what's the problem? Is everything all right?"

Kalen turned around and walked back to Dan. "No! Nothing is all right! Everything *sucks!*" he shouted. A few people turned to look in their direction, but Kalen didn't care. "What do you care about my life, anyway?" he continued. "You're a liar and a fake!"

Dan frowned. "Kalen, maybe we should go into my office," he said in a low voice.

"Why? So you can sell me some more lies, Dan? Save them for some other sucker," Kalen said furiously.

Without a word, Dan took Kalen by the arm and marched him into his office. He shut the door and sat down behind his desk. "Sit," he said, pointing at the chair opposite him.

Kalen stood in the same spot, glaring at Dan.

"I said SIT!" Dan barked.

Kalen threw himself into the leather chair and stared at Dan. Kalen clenched his jaw.

"Now, I want to know what this attitude is all about," Dan said firmly. "Spill it."

"I think you know what the problem is," Kalen spat.

"No, I don't," Dan repeated.

Kalen rolled his eyes. "I saw the website."

Dan looked puzzled. "What website?"

"The one with your picture on it. The one that sells steroids," Kalen said angrily.

Dan said nothing. "What was the name of the site?" he asked quietly.

"I don't know…Ana-bulk.com or something like that. What difference does it make?" Kalen asked. "The fact is, you've been telling me to eat a healthy diet and showing me how to bulk up. You're a liar! The whole time, you've been taking steroids! Everything you said was a lie." He folded his arms across his chest and sat back in the chair. He waited for Dan to say something.

Dan sighed heavily. "I see," he said. "You think I'm on steroids." He stood up and walked over to the glass wall. He watched the people exercising in the weight room for a moment. Then he turned around to face Kalen and said, "Kalen, I'm going to be totally honest with you."

"Why start now?" Kalen sneered.

Dan gave him a stern look. "Listen carefully. It's true. I *did* use steroids when I was competing." He paused for a moment. "That's a difficult thing for me to admit. But I think you need to know the whole truth. After the first eight months of training, my trainer gave me a handful of pills. He said they would make me perform better. He said it was the only way I could compete with the top bodybuilders.

I didn't know any better, Kalen," Dan said, his face serious. "I had no idea that those drugs would harm me or how bad they could hurt my body. I trusted my trainer, so I took them."

Kalen shook his head. "I don't believe this."

"At first, it was fantastic. I was thrilled. I got better results than ever before," Dan continued. "I was winning competitions all over the world. But it wasn't long before I started getting some of the side effects. My muscles ached, I couldn't sleep, and I broke out in the worst case of acne. It was all over my back and shoulders. I had to take another drug to clear up the pimples."

Kalen suddenly thought of Scott's back that day in the locker room. He'd called it a rash, but it had looked exactly like zits.

"So what happened?" Kalen asked.

"I stopped taking the steroids," Dan replied. "I stopped competing, too. I realized that looking good wasn't worth it if I was damaging my body. Now I know that I don't have to take steroids to look good, either. I feel better and stronger now than I did when I was using them. That picture you saw of me on the website was taken a long time ago. My old trainer probably gave it to the company back then." He sat down and faced Kalen across his desk. "So now you know my story. Any questions?"

Kalen frowned. "Well actually, I'm worried about Scott. I think he may be using steroids."

Dan looked alarmed. "Why? Have you seen him taking them?"

Kalen shook his head. "No, but I've seen other signs." He explained about the acne, the mysterious phone call, the fight at Lee's, and how Scott had tried to hit him.

Dan looked concerned. "It sounds like Scott is experiencing the rage I was telling you about. He was probably talking to a dealer on the phone. He was asking for 'gear,' which is just another word for steroids. A 'plateau' is when a certain type of steroid stops being effective. Scott probably needs something stronger to keep bulking up."

"What's a 'dart?'" Kalen asked.

"It's a needle. Some steroids are injected. Some are taken as pills," Dan replied.

Kalen suddenly remembered something. "I found a yellow pill in the change room near our lockers. It could have been a steroid," he said. "I'm not sure."

Dan nodded. "It probably was," he said. "I think someone at the gym may be dealing steroids to some of the members."

Kalen realized Dan was referring to Karl. Karl was always lurking around and talking to

Scott. Kalen remembered how Karl had lost his temper with him that first day for leaving the weights on the floor. "Dan, do you think Karl could be selling steroids to Scott?" he asked.

"Yes. I've suspected Karl for a while. Jake has been keeping a close eye on him for weeks. I think it's time for me to talk to Scott," Dan said. "Do you know where he is?"

Kalen shook his head slowly. "No. I came here to look for him."

Dan stood up. "You'd better go home, Kalen. If Scott calls you, don't accuse him of anything. He probably needs a friend to talk to right now."

"Okay." Kalen stood up. "Listen, Dan, I'm sorry about what I said...I didn't know..."

Dan slapped Kalen on the back. "Don't worry about it. No harm done," he said with a smile. "You're a good kid, Kalen, and you're a good friend."

Kalen turned to go. "Thanks. See you later."

"Later." Dan pressed the intercom button on his telephone. "Jake, could you come to my office, please?"

chapter 17

coming clean

It was after dark when Kalen arrived at home. It was almost seven o'clock. He'd missed dinner and was hungry. He was totally wiped out. The day had been awful. On top of everything, Kalen was going to have to deal with his parents when he got inside.

Kalen tossed his jacket and backpack on the bench near the front door. He went into the kitchen. His father and Julia were up to their elbows in suds at the sink.

"Hi, Kalen! It took you long enough to get home," Julia said.

Mr. Sommers wiped his hands on a dish towel. "Your mother is in the office, Kalen. She'd like to speak with you," he said, putting a stack of plates into the cupboard.

Here we go again, Kalen thought as he headed for the office. He was sure his mother was going to ground him for another two weeks, especially when she found out he'd gone to the Sweat Shop. She would think he'd been working out when he was supposed to be grounded. He couldn't exactly tell her about his conversation with Dan.

The office door was closed. Kalen knocked lightly. "Mom?"

"Come in, dear," came his mother's voice.

Kalen opened the door. His mouth fell open. Scott was sitting in the easy chair. A glass of milk and a plate of cookies sat on the table next to him. He smiled and stood up when Kalen entered the room.

"Hey, man. I thought I'd drop by, but you weren't home. So I've been chatting with your mom. She makes a wicked chocolate chip cookie," Scott said with a grin.

"Yeah," said Kalen. He didn't know what else to say.

Mrs. Sommers cleared her throat. "Well, I'm going to check on your father and sister. They're probably making a mess of the kitchen." She slipped past Kalen. She squeezed his shoulder as she passed by. "Your dinner is in the oven, dear," she said and closed the door behind her.

Kalen and Scott stood looking at the floor. Then Kalen said, "So, what are you doing here?"

Scott looked down at the floor. "I came to say I'm sorry for the way I acted earlier. I was a total idiot."

"Yeah, you were," Kalen agreed.

Scott frowned. "Well, anyway, I'm sorry. And I'm sorry about Amber. I know you two were pretty serious."

"Yeah," Kalen mumbled.

"I told your mom you got dumped. That's why she's not giving you a hard time about being late."

"Oh. Thanks," Kalen said. "Scott, I think we should talk about some stuff."

"Like what?" Scott asked. His eyes were narrowed as he stared at Kalen.

"Like your phone call in the washroom. I know what you were talking about," Kalen said.

Scott stared at Kalen. He didn't say a word.

Kalen continued. "I know it's your body and it's your decision, but we're talking about drugs, man. You could screw up your body for the rest of your life. You could get liver cancer, or have a heart attack, or...or...your balls could shrink!"

Scott rolled his eyes at Kalen. "Okay, I get the picture."

Both boys were silent for a moment.

Kalen spoke first. "Why did you do it?"

Scott looked down at the empty glass in his hand. "I don't know."

"Come on, Scott. I'm your best friend," Kalen said.

Scott took a deep breath. "I just wanted to get big before we came back to school this year. You don't know what it's like being the little guy, Kalen," Scott said fiercely. "I have to work so hard to prove myself in every sport. Coaches always look for the big guys. Girls are a whole other problem," he said. "What girl wants to date a guy who weighs less than she does?"

He looked away. "Just once, I wanted to be noticed. I wanted people to look at me and say, wow, look at that guy. When I started using steroids, they did."

Kalen was blown away. He had always thought Scott was the most confident guy he knew. Now he realized Scott had the same fears as everybody else. *Just like me,* Kalen thought.

"So where did you get all the steroids?" Kalen asked.

Scott took a cookie. "Oh, just from a guy I know," he said.

"Is it Karl?" Kalen asked.

Scott was silent for a moment. "Yes," he said finally.

Kalen nodded. "I figured it was him. You were always talking to him at the gym." He sat down in the chair in front of the computer. "'It's not worth it, man. It isn't worth it to kill yourself for muscle."

Scott sighed heavily. "I know. It was a stupid thing to do."

"Well, I guess everyone makes mistakes," said Kalen. He slapped Scott on the back and stood up. "So, do you want to go for a burger?"

Scott grinned back. "Sure. Extra bacon, double cheese?"

Kalen nodded. "And a bun!"

By the time the boys left Lee's, things were just about back to normal. As Kalen walked home, he thought about everything that had happened over the past six weeks. He had learned things about Scott that he hadn't known before. He was sticking to his workout routine and feeling good about himself. Life was pretty good.

Upstairs in his bedroom, Kalen flicked on his computer to check his e-mail. He had two new messages. The first one was from Amber. Kalen was surprised. He didn't expect to hear from her. He thought of her pretty face and warm smile, and he felt sad. He wished things had worked out with her. Kalen read the message from Amber.

Hi, Kalen,

Even though we're not dating, I hope
we can still be friends. I think
you're a great guy. And you've
really worked hard to get in shape.
I think it's cool that you set a
goal for yourself and you reached
it. So don't forget...you still owe
me an ice cream cone.

Amber

A grin spread over Kalen's face as he read
the message. He wrote back:

Hi, Amber,

I won't forget. I promise.

Kalen

Kalen clicked "send" and sat back in his chair.
Maybe things will work out after all, he thought
with a smile.

The second message in Kalen's inbox was
still waiting to be read. The subject line
screamed at him.

GET TOTALLY RIPPED! GET AMAZING
MASS!! GET STEROIDS AT THE LOWEST
PRICES ANYWHERE!!!

Right away, Kalen hit the delete key. As far
as he was concerned, it was junk mail.

glossary

abs
The short form of "abdominal." Abdominal muscles are on a person's stomach.

anabolic
A chemical reaction in the body that results in increased physical strength

anabolic steroids
Drugs that have an effect that is similar to the hormone testosterone (see below). Anabolic steroids are said to help an athlete perform better, but they are against the law and have deadly side effects.

barbell
A long bar with weight added to both ends. It is held or lifted with two hands.

biceps
A muscle in the inside of the upper arm, between the shoulder and the elbow

bulking up
To gain size and mass by eating as much as one can while training as hard as possible

carbohydrate
A molecule that serves as the body's main short-term source of fuel. Carbohydrates are found in fruits, vegetables, and starchy foods like pasta.

creatine
A chemical that naturally occurs in muscle tissue. Creatine provides energy to the body. It is also sold as a powder. Some bodybuilders add this powder to their diet to increase the amount of creatine in their muscles. They believe it helps them perform short, high-intensity exercise.

dumbbell
A short bar with weight added to both ends that can be held or lifted with one hand

lat muscle
The short form of *latissimus dorsi*. This Latin term means "lateral muscles of the back."

metabolism
A process that occurs in the body. It determines how a person's body breaks down the food he or she eats. It also helps determine one's weight.

pecs
The short form of *pectorialis major*. Pecs are the two large muscles on the front of the chest.

plateau

The point after a period of improvement or growth when things even out. With steroid use, it is the point when the drug no longer has an effect and no further improvement or muscle growth occurs. Users then start taking more steroids to get an effect. This is dangerous because the side effects can also get worse.

ripped

This word describes a state of very low body fat with high muscle separation. Muscles can be seen easily through the skin. Also called "cut" and "sliced."

'roid rage

An outburst of anger and violence shown by anabolic steroid users

supplement

Any substance that is added to one's diet. Most supplements are simply nutrients that the body usually gets from food.

testosterone

The primary male sex hormone. Most anabolic steroids are made up of chemicals that are similar to testosterone.

Do you want to read more
about Bayview High?

Turn the page
for a sneak preview!

turn the page for
a sneak preview
of

DANGEROUS
RIVALS

A.D. Fast

chapter 1

king of the road

"It's a piece of junk," Shawn said matter-of-factly. He hit the hood of the '94 truck with his hand. It was a navy blue 4 X 4, covered in rust. The rubber liner around the driver's side door was hanging out. The fan belt needed tightening. The plugs were old, and there was a crack in the windshield. It was a piece of junk. A big, heavy 4 X 4 piece of junk. And Shawn loved it.

"Four hundred. No more," Shawn offered.

The man scratched his greasy grey head. He threw the end of a cigarette to the ground. He was wearing jeans that hung down off his butt and a white undershirt. His gut stuck out so much that it was impossible to tuck the shirt in. He also had yellow teeth and bad breath. Shawn decided then and there never to smoke again.

"My kid isn't going to be happy," he said. "Says he could use some wheels to get him to rowing practice."

Great. Now the guy was having second thoughts, and Shawn was having a heart attack. "Really? Well, let him know that a fellow rower will take good care of it."

The man thought about it for a minute.

"So you're a rower too, huh? Four hundred dollars cash you say? Sold. But I ain't throwing in the seat covers," he almost belched.

Leopard skin seat covers. *That's too bad*, Shawn thought to himself. *I'm sure the girls would love them.* Shawn wondered how bad the seat covers were if that guy sat on them every day.

"I'll tell you what, Mr. Dobson," Shawn offered. "Why don't you take those things off the seats now, while I remove the old license plates?"

Shawn took care of the plates. Then he stood on the man's driveway waiting to sign the papers for his new truck. He looked around the yard as he waited. The man's house was nice enough. Not small, but not huge, either. A large dog was jumping at the fence and barking. There were no other cars in the driveway. A tow truck was parked in front of the house that read "Dobson's Towing."

The man finished with the seat covers, and Shawn put his own plates on the truck. Then the guy dug around in his grubby jeans. Finally he found the right keys. Five fat fingers handed over two shiny keys. They were the keys to Shawn's freedom.

Shawn Weston had loved cars ever since he was a kid. By the age of twelve, he could do an oil change. By fourteen, he could rebuild an engine. By fifteen, he could drive. That caused a bunch of problems. By the time he turned sixteen, he wasn't allowed to drive.

Shawn had spent from age fifteen to seventeen trying to make up for taking his mom's car for a drive down the street. Thankfully, his mom's friend at the police station was the one who caught him. He could have hurt someone. As it was, all he did was drive into a pole at the Quick Mart. It was a big mistake and a dumb thing to do for a bag of chips.

Now, a year after most of his buddies, he had his license and enough money for some wheels. Driving his mom's little white car that smelled like flower spray was not great on a date. Not that Shawn had had a date in a while. Besides, he always reminded himself that even though his mom's car was not hip, it was a car. He was lucky to drive it at all.

When Shawn got into the driver's seat of his new truck, he felt like the king of the road. A king, however, without gas. It seemed Mr. Dobson forgot to fill it up.

His cell phone beeped on the car seat beside him. He turned down the crappy radio, soon to be replaced with a kicking CD player, and answered the phone.

"Yeah, Shawn here," he said into the phone.

"Don't answer the phone while you're driving, butthead," the voice on the phone said.

Shawn laughed. "If I'd known it was you I wouldn't have. Besides, how did you know I was driving?" he asked.

"Your mom told me you were probably on your way," Big Dog answered.

"Then if you knew I was driving you shouldn't have called me!" Shawn laughed. "What's up, Big Dog?"

"I'm at the school. Mr. Kennedy wants to know if his hard drive is ready. He wants to do some work tonight," the gruff voice on the other end answered. "He's right here. I told him I knew your cell number."

"Tell him it's done, and I'll bring it by in about an hour," Shawn answered. He waved to a friend out the window. "And by the way, I got the truck, thanks for asking."

Big Dog sounded surprised. "No crap? Sweet. I'll be in the gym for a while. When you drop off Kennedy's computer, come and get me. Now get off the phone, dope, it isn't safe to talk and drive."

Shawn clicked off the phone and threw it back on the dark blue seat beside him, still laughing at his friend. Big Dog would work out like a dog, and still he would only be five-foot-two. No one had the heart to tell him that no matter how strong he got, he wasn't getting any taller.

Big Dog—also known as Mark Massoff—spent a lot of time at the school and the rest of his time on the water. The Bayview High rowing team had their eyes on the Royal Cup Regatta. This year, their boat would win the medal. The entire crew was focused on winning. They swore that those weenies at Lincoln High were finally going down.

Shawn headed for home to pick up the computer for Mr. Kennedy. Shawn worked on computers to make money. He had a reputation at his high school for being fast and being good. He could rebuild a computer like he could rebuild the engine of a car. He thought they were a lot alike. Both drove something powerful and both broke down a lot.

The kicker was, Shawn could make better money fixing computers than he could fixing cars. Trying to collect money from your butt-head friends after you've spent all Saturday on their car was hard. Collecting from desperate teachers or parents when their computers broke down was easy. No one wanted to make their favorite computer whiz angry. Especially when his prices were much better than anyone else's.

Computer *whiz*. Shawn liked that term. Computer *geek* was a thing of the past.

Shawn Weston was a six-foot-three brick wall. Computers kept him in the money. Rowing kept him in shape. He was built like a truck and had the reputation of being quiet but tough. His light brown hair was cut short. A tiny scar over his left eyebrow didn't hurt his image at all.

The truck rumbled into the driveway of his house. His younger stepbrother, Steve, came crashing out the door.

"Great car, Shawn," he yelled over from the porch, hands on his hips and eyes wide. "You have to take me for a spin in that baby!"

Shawn laughed. "Sure, Stevie. And it's a truck, not a car." He shook his head as he passed Steve on his way into the small white house.

"Yeah, truck. Right, man," Steve said as he followed Shawn through the door. Steve always looked up to Shawn. He was twelve and would do anything to impress his older brother.

"Are you coming to my soccer game tonight? We haven't lost a game yet, you know. This could be one of our last games," said Steve.

"Are you kidding? I'm your good luck charm," Shawn called down from upstairs. "I'll be there, but I might be late. I'll give you a lift home in my truck after the game."

He didn't really want to go to every single game, but his little brother was used to having him there. Steve was so proud when Shawn showed up. He tried to make it to Steve's games whenever he could.

Shawn grabbed the hard drive from Mr. Kennedy's computer. Then he grabbed a t-shirt and shorts for a quick workout in the school's weight room. When he was done, he jumped back into his truck.

He decided to get the truck washed before stopping by the school. He hoped he wouldn't lose too much of the rust on the doors when it was washed. There wouldn't be much of the truck left.

chapter 2

this means war!

Shawn parked his truck out in front of Bayview High. It was nearly five o'clock, and it was still pretty light outside. Shawn noticed that the spring days seemed to be getting longer and longer.

Most of the students had gone for the day. The only cars left in the parking lot belonged to teachers, coaches, and a few girls on the basketball team. Other than that, the school looked pretty deserted.

Shawn parked close to the main doors. He jumped out of his truck and took out the hard drive that he had repaired for Mr. Kennedy.

Big Dog was just inside the school entrance and opened the door when he saw Shawn coming. He was wearing a torn black t-shirt with the name of some heavy metal band on it, and a pair of sweat shorts. He smelled terrible.

"Man, Big Dog, you reek!" Shawn said as he walked into the school.

"Thanks, man," Big Dog answered. He considered stinking after a workout to be a compliment. "Kennedy is waiting for you in the computer lab. Did you bring your sweats?"

"Aren't you done your workout yet?" Shawn asked.

"My workouts are never done!" Big Dog answered. "Meet me in the weight room when you're done with Kennedy."

The boys stopped in front of the trophy case. They stared at the rowing trophies and checked out all the names. The last time a Bayview High rowing crew won a trophy was five years ago.

"This is going to be the year that we rule. I can just feel it," said Big Dog.

Shawn walked down the hall to the computer lab. He planned to get the computer set up, test it out, and then have a quick workout. Shawn looked forward to finishing up quickly. Mr. Kennedy always paid in cash, and Shawn was on empty. The cash would pay for gas for his new truck.

Suddenly, he heard the squeal of tires coming from the parking lot.

"Shawn, our friends are here again!" Big Dog called from down the hall. Shawn put down the hard drive and ran toward the main doors. With all the teachers in the school, no one was around to see this—again.

Five guys from the Lincoln High rowing crew were standing there. One guy was spray painting "LOSERS" on the side of the school in red paint. They all jumped back into a big, old Chevy just as Shawn and Big Dog ran through the doors.

The car pulled away, leaving skid marks on the pavement. One of the guys gave Shawn a wave and smiled. The car screeched to a stop long enough for him to yell out the window.

"Just thought we'd set the mood for the regatta, losers! But it looks like someone beat us here." He looked at his friend. "Who would spray paint on the school, Dobson?" he asked.

"I don't know. That's a very bad thing to do," another guy yelled out. "Hey, Westie, nice truck," he added, looking at Shawn. Then they sped off down the street.

Shawn ran toward his truck. He walked around to the passenger side. There was a big, red paint stripe down the entire side.

Find out what happens
to Shawn and his crew
when they take on
Lincoln High

in

DANGEROUS
RIVALS

Special Thanks

Tea Leaf Press gratefully acknowledges the help of Gary Osmond, Kerri Wall-Wilson, Ingrid Krahn, and the many other educators for their contribution of time, talent, and treasure. Their willingness to assist in making these books for children was truly inspiring.

Thank you to Ron Voth, Rick Fast, Daniel Fast, and the many other students who read entire manuscripts to help ensure the stories were interesting and accessible.

We give our most heartfelt thanks to our partners and families, who did everything from proofreading, printing, and collating to making sure that life at home continued to function. Your support was amazing. We would not have made it without you. Thank you to John Evoy, Ron Fast, Peter & Katie Fast, Peter Hough, Barbara & George Hough, Marj & Mike Levigne, Kevin Levigne, Leslie Perry, Ursula Sotzek, and Sam Turton.

Finally, we wish to extend a most sincere thank you to Ben Kooter and Vanwell Publishing for the opportunity to make our dream a reality.

BAYVIEW HIGH

Dangerous Rivals

The biggest rowing event of the year is coming up. Bayview's rivalry with another high school gets out of control.

Muscle Bound

Competition for sports is tough. Everyone is looking for an edge. How far is Kalen Sommers prepared to go?

After Dinner Barf

There's a bad seed causing trouble at Bayview High. Fighting. Stealing. Starving. It's enough to make you want to throw up

Dear Liz

Liz Gordon agreed to write an advice column for the Bayview High newspaper. She never expected romance!

Beating Up Daniel

Cool friends. Parties. Plans for a bloody beating. Justin has to make a decision. Will he become a target himself?

**Check out our website
for the latest
at Bayview High**

TEA
LEAF
PRESS

www.tealeafpress.com